THE PEW MAKER

LAURA HERN

I hope you enjoy! Blessings, Laura

Laura Hern

CONTENTS

INTRODUCTION

Maggie King had no time for love in her life. Managing Partners Mountain Cafe took all her energy.

Then the attorney's letter arrived.

She never believed in love at first sight...until she met the handsome lawyer, Ethan Reynolds.

Little did the two know that a journey of secrets, loves, and mistaking identities would change their lives forever.

CHAPTER 1

Maggie dreaded long drives. Growing up in Summerhill, Minnesota, she had been spared from the stress of traffic, crowded freeways, and the angry commuters coming and going from the Twin Cities. Her hometown had two stop lights, one on either end of the main street. Her family's restaurant, Partners Mountain Cafe, was nestled between the small post office and the bank. It was the best location in town because regular patrons could park on either side of the street.

She was heading up north to the small town of French Lake unexpectedly. She considered the three-hour drive on two-lane roads in the backwoods of Minnesota a waste of time and a nuisance.

Maggie clicked the Bluetooth earpiece.

"Hello, Mom. How was the lunch rush today?"

"Um, it was okay," Juanda King answered slowly. "But we did have a slight problem."

Maggie heard the hesitation in her mother's voice. She pulled onto the side of the road to focus on the call. She knew something was up and it wasn't pleasant.

"What happened?"

"The main oven went on the fritz, again."

Maggie sighed and rolled her eyes. "Did you call Mike to repair it?"

"Yes, but he said it's beyond repair. Your Dad and I bought that more than twenty years ago, honey. It's worn out."

"I know."

Finances at the restaurant were tight. The last thing she needed was to purchase a new commercial oven.

"Maggie, you know this building is old. The wiring needs updating, the roof is leaking…"

"Yes, Mom, I'm very aware of the repairs we need to do," she snapped, mid-sentence.

There was a brief silence.

"Let's talk about it when you get back, okay?"

Maggie smiled. "I'm sorry, Mom. I'm still confused and upset that I have to go to French Lake."

"I'm curious, too. Let me know what you find out. Love you, Magpie."

"You know that nickname reminds me of Dad. Thanks for making me smile."

Maggie ended the call, turned on the car blinker, and resumed her drive. Her GPS said she was only fifteen minutes away from her destination.

A light snow had begun as she entered the town. French Lake was smaller than Summerhill. There were no stop lights. Only three-blocks of old brick buildings and a gas station/bait shop.

She needed a pit-stop and coffee before heading to the address she had been given. She pulled into the gas station, parked, and went inside.

"Hello there, stranger," she heard almost before she could get through the door. "What can I help you with?"

Maggie stopped and looked around the small convenience store to find the voice. She saw no one standing at the counter.

She walked past a few aisles, a lottery machine, and over to the counter. "Hello? Is anyone here?"

"Be with you in a minute," she heard the voice say again. "Take a look around. Our pizza oven is broken, though."

She didn't want to look around. The counter was cluttered with a large cash register that filled one entire end. There was a small opening to pay for any purchases or gas, and the remaining counter space was stacked with what looked like prizes from a county fair.

She smiled when she saw the bubble gum cigars and cigarettes. She picked up a pack that said King's candy cigarettes.

"These would be cute for the cafe!"

"I'll have to card you if you want to buy those," a male voice boomed behind her.

Startled, she dropped the box on the floor, then quickly bent down to pick it up and put it back in the display.

Turning around quickly, she saw a tall man staring down at her. His dark green eyes seemed to sparkle in amusement.

"I'm sorry. I didn't hear you behind me," Maggie stuttered, trying hard to turn her eyes away from his gaze. "If the candy is broken, I'm happy to pay for it."

The man's mouth turned up on one side and he chuckled. "No need if you tell me your name."

Her mouth went dry and her lips stuck to her teeth as she tried to speak. She knew her cheeks were red. She took a deep breath, trying to regain her composure.

"I'm Maggie. And you are?"

"Ethan. I own this little establishment. It's not much, but it serves our little community."

They shook hands. She could not keep her eyes off him. And she knew that he knew it!

"How can I help you?"

"Well, I needed a stop before heading on. Maybe some coffee?"

Ethan chuckled. "Heading on? If you go much further, you'll be in Canada."

"I'm meeting someone here in French Lake."

"Really? I know everyone. Maybe I can point you in the right direction."

Finally, she moved her eyes off the handsome stranger standing in front of her. "I don't think I'll get lost but let me get the address from my phone."

She put the fanny pack she was carrying on the counter, opened it and took out her phone. She swiped a finger across the face and it came to life.

"I'm going to 101 Moose Run Lane. Are you familiar with that?"

Ethan blinked in surprise.

"Are you sure that's the address?"

"Yes. I received a letter from an attorney telling me to be here today for some estate issue."

Ethan took a long breath and let it out slowly.

"Are you Ms. King? Ms. Margaret King?"

She frowned. "How do you know my name?"

Pausing to take a step back, Ethan put his hands on his hips. "Because I'm the attorney who sent the letter. I'm Ethan Reynolds of The Northwoods Law Firm."

CHAPTER 2

Maggie was rarely speechless. As a young girl, her Dad had nicknamed her Magpie because she talked all the time. But at this moment, standing in a convenience store, staring in disbelief at a perfect stranger, her mouth was wide open and for the life of her, she couldn't get any words to come out.

Ethan, too, was at a loss. Finally, he shook his head slightly as if awakening from a nap. "This is surreal. I thought you would be older."

Her eyebrows lowered and her mouth tightened into a small slit.

"An older woman? Who are you?"

"I didn't mean to insult you! You're a beautiful younger...I mean you're definitely not an old lady...um, what I meant was..."

Maggie crossed her arms, trying hard not to laugh as she watched him desperately searching for words to apologize.

"I thought since Tony was older, that you would be closer to his age, that's all," he sighed.

"I don't know any Tony or why you sent me the letter."

"I'm a bit confused myself. I think it's best if we head over to his house."

"His house?"

"101 Moose Run Lane. Let me close up the store and you can follow me."

Ethan locked the cash register, turned off a few lights, and locked the front doors from the inside. He motioned for Maggie to follow him out the back door and locked it once they were outside.

"My car is parked in front, next to yours," he said as he started walking around the building.

"Why did we go out the back if you are parked in front?"

"I always park in front to make it look like customers are in the store," he grinned as he continued walking. "And the front door only locks from the inside."

Maggie rolled her eyes. Questions were racing through her mind at the speed of light. She didn't like being caught off-guard.

They reached their cars at the same time. As she slid behind the wheel, she glanced at the vehicle next to hers and noticed Ethan smiling back at her. She shivered goose bumps flecked her arms. She quickly turned her head and raised her hand to check the review mirror.

"For Pete's sake," she said aloud. "Get a grip! You don't even know him!"

For the next few minutes, she followed him down narrow dirt roads and around sharp curves. The tall evergreen trees on both sides of the road refused to let in any sunlight and cast dark shadows over her car.

He signaled and pulled off the road next to a large metal gate, got out of his car, and walked over to her.

"We need to walk from here. This old road has too many large potholes to try and drive over it."

Maggie nodded and watched Ethan unlock the gate. He

opened it just enough for them to walk through then locked it behind him.

"Tony's house is just ahead," he said. "Please be careful. I've turned my ankle walking this old road many times."

She began walking beside him, keeping her eyes on the bumpy path in front of her.

"Why is this so far off the beaten path? Was this man a hermit or something?"

"Tony was the kindest soul I've ever known," Ethan began quietly. "He was friends with my Dad and when he passed away, Tony took me in."

A somber silence fell over the two of them as they continued walking.

"I'm sorry you lost your father. My dad died many years ago."

He stopped and put his hand on her shoulder. She turned and looked into his eyes. They were moist and glassy, just like hers.

"We both have their memories in our hearts. Don't ever forget that," Ethan said softly.

"How much farther to this house?" she asked as her voice cracked.

He smiled and pointed to a two-story, metal garage building a few yards away. "That's it."

"That's a metal pole shed," she remarked. "He lived in a barn?"

Ethan nodded as he reached into his pocket and pulled out a keychain.

"I said he was a kind, humble and modest man. Wait here while I turn on the lights."

Maggie stood at the door, wondering why in the world she'd been summoned.

The lights came on and again, she was left speechless. Her eyes opened wide as she surveyed the front of the large room. It had been designed with several individual living areas, each one comfortable and inviting. Each area was filled with the most beautiful wooden furniture she had ever seen.

Ethan stood next to her, silently watching her reactions. "It's amazing, isn't it?"

"This furniture is gorgeous," she marveled, running her fingers along the carving on the chair back. "Are those…"

"Tony loved mountains and angels," he finished her sentence. "He made every piece of furniture in this building."

She eased herself carefully into the rocking chair and leaned back. It rocked back and forth smoothly. She closed her eyes and could have rocked for hours. She stopped suddenly, opened her eyes and looked for Ethan.

Standing, she walked over to him determinedly. "This is very nice, but I'd like to know why I'm here."

His smile faded and a sadness fell over him. "Tony passed away a month ago. He left everything he owned to you."

CHAPTER 3

"What?" Maggie's face went white. "What?"

"Tony left detailed instructions for me. I was to bring you, Margaret King, here."

"But I don't know him. Why would he leave anything to me?"

"I have no idea. My instructions were to find you and bring you here."

For a few minutes, neither spoke as they tried to understand what was happening.

"He left something special for you. It's upstairs."

"Upstairs?"

"That's where he lived."

He pointed to a door in the back of the room and the two started walking toward it. He took hold of her elbow.

"The stairs are steep. Don't worry, I'm right behind you." He opened the door and turned on a small light. The narrow, wooden steps seemed to stretch upward forever. There were no handrails on either side.

She nodded and began making her way to the second

floor. Several times, she put her hand on the wall to steady herself.

There was no door at the top, only a narrow hallway that led into a larger room.

Ethan walked in front of her, turned and faced her. He held up his hand to stop her.

"I told you he was a simple man. I've been up here a few times, but he never let anyone else in."

"Okay. I don't understand what you're worried about."

He shrugged his shoulders and motioned with his hand for her to walk ahead. "After you."

She walked a few feet ahead into the room. Unlike the carefully decorated showroom below, this room had no decorations. No pictures. No mirrors. No carpeting on the floor. On one side of the room was a tiny kitchenette with a small sink, a hot plate, and a small refrigerator. Across the room was a twin bed with a wooden crate beside it as a nightstand. At the foot of the bed was a green metal trunk. The only other doors led to a small bathroom and a closet.

Maggie turned to Ethan. "I know this man was like a father to you, but I don't understand any of this."

"Tony Pontello was a Vietnam war hero. He flew airplanes during Operation Rolling Thunder," he replied. "On one mission, his plane crashed while taking off and he was badly burned." He choked back tears. "His face and hands were badly disfigured."

"That's horrible. He didn't like being around people after the accident?"

"He had a few friends, but most of his work was done anonymously."

"It's so sad. I can't imagine how lonely he was."

He cleared his throat and grinned. "Nonsense! He was the most loved man I've ever known."

She shrugged her shoulders. "Why do you say that?"

"Tony moved here when he was discharged from the service. He bought this building and slowly began making furniture. Church pews to be exact. He made pews for ministers, for weddings, for memorials. His works are in many of the churches in the Twin Cities area."

"Church pews? I didn't see any pews downstairs."

"Over the years, his reputation grew and since very few people knew what he looked like, he became known as *The Pew Maker*. The Prime Minister of Canada commissioned him to make a kneeling pew for each of his daughters' weddings." Ethan's face glowed with pride.

"Remember I told you his hands were burned in the plane crash? The scars and skin grafts left him with limited movement. Each year, he lost more and more movement because the scars tightened, causing him great pain. The cold weather of northern Minnesota hurt him. He couldn't stand to have cold air touch his face or hands. He told me once that cold air felt like thousands of needles sticking his skin. Over the years, making pews became too difficult. So, he made the furniture you saw downstairs. He donated the pieces to disabled veterans or widows of veterans."

Maggie nodded in agreement and sat on the green trunk. "I can see why he was loved by many people." She paused briefly and looked up at Ethan. "And I can see why you loved him, too."

He knelt beside the trunk. "Let's find out why Tony brought you here." He took her hand and helped her stand up. "I've never seen what's inside this trunk, even though as a kid, I asked him to open it many times."

He took another key from his pocket and put it in the trunk's lock. He jiggled the key, but the old lock wouldn't budge. He tried several times, but no luck.

He stood and threw up his hands in frustration. "It's going to take more than this little key to open the lock."

"What do you suggest we do?"

Her cell phone rang before he could answer. She took it from her fanny pack and looked at the screen. It was her Mom.

"Hey, Mom. Is everything all right?"

"Honey, I saw on the news that a snowstorm is heading your way. I don't want you to drive home tonight and get caught in it. Is there a hotel close to where you are?"

"I'm sure I will find something. Thank you for letting me know."

"Promise you will not head back tonight. I know how stubborn you can be!"

Maggie chuckled. "I promise. I won't drive back to Summerhill tonight."

"Okay. But call me tomorrow when you head out. Love you."

"Love you, too." She ended the call and turned to see the biggest grin on Ethan's face.

"What are you grinning about?"

He tried to hide his smile. "Me, grinning? Never."

"It appears that I will need a hotel room tonight. A snowstorm is heading this way. Do you know of any close by?"

He tapped his fingertips on his chin as if deep in thought. "The nearest hotel is across the Canadian border. Did you happen to bring your passport?"

"Of course not. I thought I'd be on the road back home by now."

His face took on an almost mischievous look and his smile broadened.

"You look like a Cheshire Cat that just had a canary fly into its mouth," she quipped.

"Who? Me? Nope." He paused and the wide grin began to disappear. He paced back and forth before speaking.

"Look. We want to open this trunk tonight, correct?"

"Yes. I'm anxious to straighten this out."

"I have tools," he paused and looked directly into her eyes, "and I've got a four-bedroom house. Why don't you stay with me?"

Zeus couldn't have thrown a bigger lightning bolt down from Mt. Olympus than the one that hit her stomach. The thought of being alone with him had her hormones raging. She tried to sound nonchalant.

"If you're sure there are no hotels, I guess I have no choice." She tilted her head slightly and a half smile appeared on her lips. "Besides, you may need a woman's touch." She cringed inside when she realized she had spoken out loud what her mind was thinking. "I mean help opening the trunk," she sputtered nervously, knowing that her foot was rooted squarely in her mouth.

His eyes opened wide, amused at watching her squirm. "We'd better get going. The storm's not going to wait for us to talk about a woman's touch." He laughed out loud.

"Very funny. You know what I meant!"

CHAPTER 4

W ithin a few minutes, Ethan had locked up Tony's garage home and loaded the trunk in his pickup. Maggie stood beside her car, waiting for him to give her directions.

"Ready to go?" she asked. "What's your address?" She had her cell phone out, ready to start the GPS.

He smiled in amusement. "Just follow me."

She hesitated. The snow was falling heavily now and the wind was creating swirling drifts across the ground.

"I'd rather have your address in my GPS in case I lose you."

"Lose me?" He looked surprised. "Think I'm going to drive too fast or something?"

"No," she replied curtly. "I'm not familiar with the roads. What if I get stuck in a snow drift? How would I contact you?"

He paused for a moment to think as he walked closer to her.

He looks like Perry Mason ready to drop the hammer on a guilty witness, she thought to herself.

He gently put his hand under her chin and raised her head. "I'm not going to lose you. Trust me. I'll go slow."

For a few seconds, she didn't think he was talking about driving. Her heart was beating quickly and she could feel her cheeks flush.

She didn't know if he sensed what she was feeling, but he slowly dropped his hand and took a couple steps back.

"Let's get going. My house is about a mile from here."

She nodded and watched as he walked back to his truck. She took a deep breath, blowing it out through pursed lips as she opened her door and got in. She started the car, turned off the heater, and opened the driver's side window a bit. Cold air rushed in. She closed her eyes for a second. The one thing she didn't need at this moment was more heat.

True to his word, he drove slowly and she had no problem keeping up. He turned into the driveway of a beautiful log cabin. She pulled her car next to his and quickly got out.

"Welcome to Hotel Reynolds, Ms. King," he said, bowing to her.

She nodded and pretended to curtesy. "Thank you, kind sir."

They laughed and walked up the few steps to the front door. A faded wooden sign in the shape of a moose hung next to the doorbell. It read *Reynolds*. Maggie giggled when she saw it.

"Dad was a hunter," Ethan said as he opened the door and motioned for her to go inside.

She was surprised by how cozy and calm this log cabin was. Even though the fireplace was not lit, she felt warm and strangely at home.

"I've always loved log cabins. Simple and natural," she said, gazing at the high wooden ceilings. "How long have you lived here?"

"I grew up here. This was my Mom and Dad's dream house. She said the logs provide a perfect framework, but a home is created by those who live in it."

He walked over to the fireplace and picked up a few logs that were stacked in front.

"Make yourself at home while I start a fire."

She took off her coat and fanny pack, laid them across one of the puffy armchairs. As she walked around the room, she saw antique tables, a gorgeous sideboard, and a small roll top desk. Across the top of each piece were family photos, carefully placed on lace doilies.

"These are beautiful antiques," she marveled. "Your parents were collectors?"

He threw the last log on the fire and turned to see her picking up a photo of his parents.

"These few pieces belonged to my mother's family." He walked across the room, stood beside her and gazed at the photo she was holding.

"That was taken shortly after their wedding," he remarked.

"They look so happy," she said, carefully putting the photo back on the doily.

"I can't remember a time when they weren't happy."

He sighed and swallowed hard. "Not until Mom died. Dad was lost without her."

The two fell silent. Maggie took his hand in hers and held it for just a moment. She didn't back away when his lips lightly touched hers...until the doorbell rang, jolting the two back to reality.

"Um, I'd better see who that is," he said awkwardly.

She nodded, feeling more embarrassed than she did when she tried to kiss Johnny Moore in grade school. The two had leaned forward so quickly, they bumped heads...hard. She had a red mark all through English class!

Ethan opened the door and picked up a box that had been left on the front porch. He closed the door and walked inside with a surprised grin on his face.

"I forgot that I called in pizzas when we left Tony's. Hope you're hungry...and like stuffed crust supreme. In case you don't eat meat, I ordered a veggie one, too."

She hadn't realized how hungry she was until the aroma of pizza floated in the air.

"I'm starving! What can I do to help you?"

"Let's eat in the kitchen. Follow the Hotel Reynolds' award-winning master chef!" he chuckled.

She was pleasantly surprised when she saw the kitchen. The high ceiling beams and cabinets were made of the same dark wood as the outside. A fantastic cast iron oven, complete with four ornately sculptured claw feet, covered an entire wall. There was an island with copper pots and pans hanging from a rack above it.

"Wow! This kitchen is heavenly! Your mom must have been a wonderful cook."

"Mom tried very hard," he chuckled, "but she couldn't make a peanut butter and jelly sandwich that tasted good. It just wasn't her cup of tea."

"Was your Dad a chef?"

"He was. He joked that he'd learned to cook doing KP duty when he was in the service."

He opened a cabinet door and handed her two plates to set on the island.

"Where did he serve?" she asked, putting napkins by the plates.

"Dad joined the Army back in the early 70's. He was stationed at Ft. Bragg and wanted to see action as a paratrooper. He shattered his leg on his first jump and ended up with pins in his ankle and shin. So, he became an Army Food Service Specialist."

"My goodness. Did he supervise the kitchens at the base?"

"No. But he did become an expert in peeling potatoes!"

Both laughed loudly.

"Dig in, Maggie. I'll get us both a drink."

CHAPTER 5

The two talked and laughed while they devoured the pizzas. Maggie put her napkin on the plate and pushed if forward. She leaned back in her chair and stretched her arms above her head.

"That was delicious. I'm stuffed! Thanks for ordering it."

Ethan sat back in his chair and winked at her. "I agree. I couldn't eat another bite."

"Let me help you clean up. We still need to open that trunk," she stated.

"You got it. I'll get the trunk from the pickup if you'll put these plates in the sink."

He stood up, walked over to the window and moved one side of the curtain to look out.

"It's snowing hard. There must be a half-foot all ready."

"Mom said there was a good chance of a large accumulation of that darn white stuff."

He turned from the window to see her standing with her back to him, washing dishes in the sink. She looked beautiful and he felt his heart pound. A sensation burned deep inside him and he knew he had to cool off.

"I'm going out the back door. Be back in a flash."

With her hands still in dishwater, she turned and saw him beeline out the back door.

"Was he in a hurry or what?" she said out loud.

She finished the dishes and walked to the back door, opening it as he came in with the trunk.

"You're shivering and covered with snow," she said as he sat the trunk on the floor. "For goodness sake, why didn't you wear your coat?"

Because I couldn't let you see how excited you made me feel.

"I'm a tough old bird. A little snow won't bother me."

She remembered seeing a blanket over the back of one of the puffy chairs by the fireplace. "I'm going to get a blanket from the living room for you." She hurried into the kitchen before he could protest.

He dusted himself off then picked up the trunk. It wasn't especially heavy, just bulky and wet from the snow. He walked into the kitchen and placed it on the floor in front of him.

She appeared with the blanket and draped it over his shoulders.

"Thank you, but it really wasn't necessary."

"Hey, I noticed hot cocoa mix in a jar by the oven. How about a cup before we open this thing?"

He looked at her smiling face and the burning sensation started again. "That'd be great. The cups are in the first cabinet on the right."

"Coming right up, sir!"

It only took a couple of minutes before the two were sipping on piping hot cocoa.

"Ahh…this hits the spot," he said. "I really don't know much about you, Margaret King. Tell me all about yourself."

She took a small sip and then set her cup on the island.

She glanced down at her hands and then looked up into his eyes.

"There's not much to tell. I grew up in Summerhill and had a pretty normal childhood. I played volleyball and basketball in junior high. My parents, Juanda and Nathan King, own a restaurant, Partners Mountain Cafe. I started working there after school and on weekends."

"Family-owned businesses require a huge time commitment from everyone. Did you resent having to work there?"

She picked up her cup and took a long sip. "Not at all. I enjoy cooking. My dream was to attend the Culinary Institute of America in New York and become a world renowned chef. Wolfgang Puck was my idol."

"You wanted to be one of those high society hash-slingers?"

She sat straight up in her chair, pretending to be insulted.

"I'll have you know, I can sling hash with the best of them. Wolfgang just hasn't met me yet!"

They both laughed.

"Where did you work after graduation? Did you live in New York for a time?"

He watched as her face turned white. She sat back in her chair and looked like someone had knocked the wind out of her.

"I'm sorry. I've somehow upset you with my nosey questions." He leaned forward and put his hand on her right knee.

She slowly shook her head. She took her left hand and rubbed the back of her neck.

"My dad died during my first year of culinary school. We weren't wealthy people, and my mom couldn't run the restaurant on her own. I left school to help her."

"Do you have brothers or sisters who could've helped?"

She shook her head. "I'm an only child."

He took his hand off her knee and sat back in his chair.

"I understand. We have more in common than you think. I'm an only child, too. I wanted to be an automotive engineer and work in Detroit for Ford or Chevrolet."

"What happened?"

"My Mom's dream was for me to have a career in law. During my senior year of high school, she was diagnosed with cancer. I promised her I would become an attorney. She passed away during my third year of law school. I had to finish, for her sake."

"And you came back to French Lake to practice law?"

He chuckled. "Yes and no. Dad had purchased the gas station in town and after mom died, he lost interest in it. We tried to sell it, but there were no takers. I moved in with him and started a small law business I could do from home. It gave me time run the store."

She nodded. "The Northwoods Law Firm."

"Yes. Big name for only a one-man show."

"Seems we do have a few things in common, Mr. Reynolds."

They finished their cocoa and sat staring at the trunk.

He finally broke the silence. "Do you want to open this or wait till morning?"

She sighed. Her thoughts had been focused on the handsome man sitting across from her. She hadn't thought about the trunk or its contents in hours. She knew that once they opened that trunk, she'd have no reason to stay.

"Think it can wait till morning?" she asked.

He rose from his chair and took both of her hands in his.

"That's what I was hoping you'd say," his voice was quiet and raspy. "Maggie, I've been drawn to you since I first saw you."

She opened her lips to speak, but all she could do was stare into his eyes. Her heart was racing and it was hard breathe.

"It's been a very long time since…"

Pulling her closer to him, he slowly let go of her right hand and raised his fingers to gently push her hair away from her face.

"It has for me, too." His hand brushed her cheek and his words were so soft, an unbearable shiver ran through her.

It took all of her strength to pull her eyes from his gaze. "We've only just met and you barely know me," she said, desperately trying not melt into his arms. "I've been hurt before and I'm not ready for another relationship."

He could hear loneliness in her voice…and fear. He was holding her so tightly, he knew she could feel the fire that burned through his veins. He pictured her lips pressed against his and his pulse quickened.

He let go of her and stepped back slightly. Her body ached to touch him.

"I am not the type of man that would ever cause you pain," he said slowly. "I've been hurt by love, too." He stood, rolled his shoulders and cleared his throat.

"We need to see what's so important about this trunk," he sighed, negating his former suggestion. "What do you say? Should we open it?"

She nodded and took a few breaths, thankful he had given her a way out of their conversation.

CHAPTER 6

"Let me get a few tools and we'll have this lock open in no time," Ethan said. "I'll be right back."

She watched as he walked over to one of the kitchen cabinets and opened the bottom drawer. He took a small, red toolbox from the drawer before closing it.

"Your Dad let you keep your tools in the kitchen?" she questioned him.

He laughed as he removed a couple of items from the box. "Absolutely not! He'd have a cow if he knew I stored them here. Never underestimate the need for a long screwdriver, hammer, and duct tape!"

"Tools of the trade every attorney needs, I suppose."

"If it works, I'll use it." He handed her the duct tape. "Hold this please."

She took the tape and added, "Think you can get that lock open with those tools?"

He smirked. "Oh, ye of little faith! I'll get this bugger open if it takes all night."

She watched as he put the screwdriver in the lock and started hitting it with the hammer. She couldn't help staring at his face. Each time he struck the handle end of the screwdriver with the hammer, the muscles in his jaw tightened and loosened. His eyebrows grew close together. She was mesmerized by the movement of his lips. He frowned. He grunted. He groaned and bit his lip. She couldn't turn her eyes away until she heard a loud crack.

"We got it!" He said, wiping a little bit of sweat from his brow. He put the tools and the remaining pieces of the lock on the counter.

"Why don't you open it?" he grinned. "It is your trunk."

She hesitated and for a brief moment, not sure she wanted to see what was hidden inside.

She took a deep breath. "Here goes."

The lid of the trunk squeaked as it opened to reveal what it had carefully hidden for so long. The two leaned over to look inside. There was a manilla envelope on top of what appeared to be a layer of butcher paper. Written on it were the words, "Maggie King. Read this first."

She picked up the envelope and glanced at Ethan. He shrugged his shoulders and looked as confused as she felt.

The tape on the back seal of the envelope came off easily. She opened the envelope and took out a letter that had a photo clipped to it. Her eyes widened and her mouth fell open. A young airman and a beautiful young girl stood smiling, looking into each other's eyes.

"Who is this man?" she asked him. Her voice quivered as she took off the paper clip.

He took the photo from her hand and studied it. "Why, that's Tony! Look how young and handsome he was."

He looked at her and was startled by her expression. "What's wrong?"

She closed her eyes, raised her hand to her cover her mouth, and began pacing back and forth in front of him.

He stood up to stop her from pacing. "What on earth is wrong?"

Tears began to fill her eyes. "The girl in that photo is my mother."

"What?" he stammered, letting go of her shoulders. "Are you sure?"

She slunk onto one of the kitchen chairs and nodded. "I've seen her high school yearbook pictures. That's her."

The two were silent, gathering their own thoughts and not knowing what to say. She looked down at the letter she was still holding and raised it as if she were going to read it.

"I can't read this right now. Would you please?"

He looked into her eyes and saw a frightened, lost little girl. He took the letter from her hands and began reading.

Dear Maggie,

I'm sure you're confused and wondering why you're here. Or what this old man's life had to do with yours. I hope Ethan is sitting beside you as you read this letter. He's a good man and I knew you would need a strong shoulder to lean on.

Please be patient with me. I've thought about how I could share my thoughts with you many times. Now that I'm writing this, my heart is in my throat and tears are running down my face. My words don't seem to be enough.

My name is Anthony Pontello. Everyone has always called me Tony. I grew up in a small Texas town and dreamed of becoming a fighter pilot like my father. He was killed during a routine training mission in New Mexico. Years later, my mother married a banker and moved to Saint Paul, Minnesota.

I joined the air force in 1967 during the Vietnam war. I worked hard to become one of the youngest pilots in the service at the time.

I had been training other pilots for several years and was long overdue for furlough. In the fall of 1972, I had a month's furlough and spent much of it with my mother. During a visit to North

Shore, I stopped at the Maritime Visitor's center in Duluth. It was there I met and fell in love with Juanda James.

She was visiting a girlfriend that weekend and decided to stop at the center before leaving Canal Park. She was walking in as I was leaving. We bumped into each other, and the moment I looked into her beautiful brown eyes, I fell in love with her. I realize that sounds cliche', but we both felt an uncontrollable passion for each other from the beginning.

We walked and talked. We spent hours on the Lakefront that day. This photo was taken at a restaurant by the water. Can you see how much in love we were? I knew in deep in my soul that we would live together forever. She felt the same.

We spent every moment we could together. She was a senior in high school and we planned to marry once she graduated.

I was shipped overseas when my leave was over. I remember how beautiful she looked as we said goodbye in the airport. I wanted our goodbye kiss to last forever. But it didn't. It couldn't. Suddenly, I was walking to the plane and she waving to me.

She promised to write every day. I promised to answer every day. But once I got back to the base, my duties kept me busy and I rarely found time to write. At first, Juanda sent three letters a week.

On January 3, 1973, our lives changed forever. My squad had a practice mission scheduled early that morning. I did my usual routine, checking the plane, checking everything. I sat in the pilot seat and felt a strange, uncomfortable feeling. Almost a premonition if you will. My co-pilot sat down and I turned to face him to start our pre-flight routine. Before I could say anything, I heard alarms screaming all around me. What followed was a blur for many years and even today, I don't remember every detail.

I was told that one of the engines had exploded and a fireball engulfed the cockpit. Before the medics could get us out of the plane, both my copilot and I suffered third-degree burns over much of our bodies.

It was several weeks before I was lucid enough to open my eyes.

My ears were badly burned and for months, all I could hear was a loud ringing. My copilot had died while I was unconscious. I will spare you the terrible difficulties of healing from massive burns. I don't remember how many skin grafts, skin scrapings, and surgeries were performed on me. My hands and face were badly disfigured. I glanced in a mirror only once during my time in the hospital. The face that stared back at me was horrific and unrecognizable. Devastated, I vowed to never look in a mirror again.

I was hospitalized for a little over two years and trying to recover enough to live my life once more. Dreams of Juanda kept me motivated during those long months of rehab. Yet, during that time, I hadn't received any mail. Not from my family. Not from Juanda. I became depressed, and for a time, lost the will to keep fighting.

Ethan stopped and glanced up to check on Maggie's reaction to this news. She had a blank look in her eyes and no expression on her lips.

"Why don't we take a break from this," he said. He stood, laid the letter on the island, and walked behind her chair. He put his hands on her shoulders.

She kept shaking her head slightly. "I'd like a drink of water, please."

"You bet." He patted her and walked to the sink to fill two glasses of water. He turned back to see that she had picked up the letter and was staring down at it.

"Take a drink of this," he said, holding the glass in front of her. She took the glass and a small sip while he took his seat across from her.

"Why didn't my Mother ever mention him?" Maggie asked.

Ethan shook his head. "As far as I know, he never married. He never mentioned anyone named Juanda."

"We need to finish this letter."

"Want me to continue reading?"

She took a deep breath and said, "No. I want to finish this." Her voice cracked when she began reading where he had left off.

A few weeks before I was to be released, an air force officer walked into my room. He was carrying a brown briefcase and had a stoic look about him. He showed no emotion as he explained to me that an error had been made shortly after the accident.

The officer apologized, but said in the chaos of the moment, my tags were lost. Somehow, the copilot's remains were mistaken for mine. My parents were notified that I had died in the accident.

Maggie's hand flew to her mouth. "His family thought he was dead. That's awful!"

"Tony rarely had visitors and he never talked about any family. I'm so sorry for him."

She nodded. "There's a little more in the letter. It's just so sad."

The air force was sorry for the mix-up and did everything in their power to correct what had happened. My parents had passed away thinking I had died. He then gave me a key to a green trunk that had been delivered to my room.

Inside were some of my personal belongings that I thought had been lost. And there were two unopened letters...both from Juanda.

At the sight of her letters, my heart pounded and I couldn't wait to hold her again. The first letter told me how happy she was and that she couldn't wait to see me again. But the second brought a harsh reality.

She wrote that she was pregnant and very happy. That she couldn't wait for me to come home and we could be married. The date on the letter was January 3, 1973...the same day as the plane fire. My heart sank. I was sick to my stomach. I'd been injured before either of the letters were delivered and two long years had passed.

When I was discharged, I headed to Summerhill to find her and explain everything. I drove to a little café where I'd been told she worked. As I pulled into the parking lot, she was standing outside the entrance. She looked more beautiful than I remembered. I looked in the rearview mirror at my horrible features. Would she recognize me? Would she still love me? Am I the father of a girl or boy?

I gathered my courage and opened the car door. But I stopped before standing up. A handsome man had parked next to me. He got out and took the most beautiful little girl I've ever seen from the car. As they walked toward the cafe, Juanda ran forward to meet them. The little girl called her mama.

Juanda hugged and kissed the man. I felt like my heart was being ripped from my chest. I couldn't breathe. I watched as they went inside the café. I slowly closed the car door and cried. It was more painful than any of the burns or treatments.

I looked again in the review mirror and knew that I could never try to contact her. I loved her too much to ruin her life.

I moved to French Lake where I could be a short distance from Summerhill. As you look through this trunk, dear Margaret, know that I have always loved you. I was in the audience when your first-grade class sang during the school Christmas program. I watched as you played sports. And I know that you left college to take care of your Mother.

I'm so proud of the woman you have become! I know you must be feeling hurt, confused, betrayed perhaps. None of this was your mother's fault. Whether you knew of me or not, please do not blame her. She did the best she could to give you a good life and to teach you to love.

Ethan, I hope you experience the great love that I was lucky to find. Who knows? She could be sitting in front of you right now.

Love, Tony.

The two didn't speak for several moments.

Maggie held the letter tightly, trying to grasp everything she had just read. She put the letter down and reached inside the trunk to remove the butcher paper layer. Two black boxes were on top of two or three scrapbooks.

She opened one of the boxes and gasped. "It's a Purple Heart! He was awarded the Purple Heart!" She carefully handed it to Ethan.

"Oh my gosh," he smiled. "He never mentioned it. What's in the other blue box?"

She opened the other box. "This is the Distinguished Flying Cross! I know that is awarded for outstanding heroism demonstrated during a flight or mission," she sighed. "He truly was a hero."

She carefully closed the medal box and turned her attention to the scrapbooks. They were labeled with her name and the years it covered. Each one held precious photos of her from elementary school through high school. There were newspaper clippings of every award she'd earned.

"He must have spent years putting these together," she marveled.

Ethan nodded. "What's under that last scrapbook? It's some sort of box?"

She moved the last scrapbook to find a small box with carvings on the top and sides. It had a small metal latch in the front, but it was not locked.

"That looks like a jewelry box or something," she said. "The angels on top resemble those on that rocker I saw. Do you think he made this?"

He took the box and studied the outside. "I'm sure he did. I've seen these angels on some of the wedding pews he made, too."

He sat the box down and carefully lifted the lock. Inside was a small note and a key.

"Tony left you one more note," he said as he handed her the box. "What does it say?"

She took the note from the box, unfolded it, and read silently.

"Hey, come on now, read it out loud," he urged her.

"It says he left something for me at the Lutheran church in Summerhill," she said, handing him the note. "See for yourself."

He took the note and read it out loud.

Maggie, take this key to Trinity Lutheran Church in Summerhill. Ask to speak with Harvey Milner.

CHAPTER 7

Maggie glanced at Ethan. She was suddenly exhausted.

"What time is getting to be? I was so wrapped up I lost track of time!"

He yawned and stretched his hands above his head.

"I am, too. Think we should call it a night?"

She sat forward in her chair and held her hands out toward him. He leaned forward to take her hands.

"You've been very kind to go through this with me. I'm sure it's not the regular duties of an estate attorney."

He squeezed her hands and smiled. "It's been a pleasure… and I'll be sending you a bill for these overtime hours."

They both laughed. She tried to pull her hands away, but he held on to them.

"About earlier this evening," he began, still holding her hands.

She couldn't help but stare into his eyes. It was as if he had hypnotized her.

"Let's talk about it in the morning, okay? I have a lot to think about." She pulled harder and he let go of her hands.

"Right," he muttered. "I'll put things back in the trunk for you. Let me show you to the guest room."

She nodded. She put the note back in the carved box to carry it with her. Walking through the living room, she paused in front of the fireplace for a moment.

"Are you cold?" he asked.

"Can we sit here for a little while? The fire is so warm. Do you mind?"

"We can sit here as long as you wish. Which chair do you want?"

"How about right here?" she asked as she sat down on the floor.

"It's the best seat in the house," he answered as he sat beside her.

He touched her cheek lightly. "What are you thinking?"

She looked into his eyes and felt he could see into her very soul.

She sighed and leaned into his arms. "I'm trying to process how difficult it was for my mother. It must have broken her heart to not hear from Tony after she told him she was pregnant."

He pulled her closer. "Tony loved her deeply. It's sad he never got to tell her about the accident...or meet you in person."

She reached up and pulled his face toward hers.

She couldn't control her burning desires any longer. She leaned into him and with wanton desire kissed his lips. She could feel his warmth and knew he could feel hers. She pulled back enough to gaze into his eyes and lightly trace his lips. He groaned as she softly pressed her lips to his neck. She could feel his pulse racing as her nose gently brushed his jaw. She knew he wanted her and her heart beat faster. Her breathing quickened, matching his.

Ethan kissed her with an urgency she had never experienced. He took her face in his hands and pressed his lips to hers with a fierceness she didn't recognize. The world stopped turning. All he could imagine was kissing her and lying next to her for the rest of his life.

He pulled her back gently. His face was flushed and moist from sweat. His breath slowed and he took a deep breath.

"I want you, Maggie. And I can feel that you want me too."

She knew what he was going to say, but she didn't have the strength to pull away from him.

"It's been a very emotional day," he said. "I know it sounds crazy, but I've fallen in love with you at first sight. The last thing I want is for you to wake up in the morning, when your mind is clearer, and have regrets."

She leaned in to kiss him once more, but he stopped her. He took another deep breath and gently moved her off his lap.

"I don't want to hurt you," he stood, "and I don't want to be hurt either." He recognized the disappointment in her eyes for he was battling the same emotions. He put his hands out to help her up. She tried to speak, but her mind wouldn't form words.

"Let's get some sleep. I'll fix breakfast for us and we can head over to the church in Summerhill. Okay?"

She nodded, still trying to slow her breath. She followed him to the spare bedroom.

"Goodnight, Maggie," he said before turning to walk away.

She wanted to run to him, hold him tight, and kiss him once more. But she knew she shouldn't.

"Night, Ethan." She walked into the bedroom and closed the door. She turned on the light and saw a king size bed. She walked over and felt the comforter.

She plopped on top of the bed. The day's events must

have affected her more than she'd thought. The next thing she knew, the smell of bacon was floating through the air.

Realizing she had slept through the night, she got up and looked around the room for a mirror. She saw a separate bathroom and headed there to freshen up.

CHAPTER 8

"The bacon smells wonderful," Maggie said, wondering how awkward the conversation would be after last night. "How long have you been up?"

Nathan sat a plate of hot bacon on the island in front of her. "I didn't sleep well, so I've been cooking since about 3 am." He opened the refrigerator and took out a large, covered dish, sour cream, and hot sauce.

"Your breakfast this morning includes a Sausage and Egg Bake Casserole, fresh spinach and basil pesto, homemade crescent rolls with honey butter, and coffee or cranberry juice," he paused and smiled widely. "And for dessert, Irish Coffee."

She blinked her eyes several times and picked up a slice of bacon. "My goodness! There's enough food here to feed an army!"

"My Dad always said it was better to make too much than not enough."

"It's delicious." Their eyes met and for a split second, she felt her pulse quicken and her cheeks flush.

"Dig in. We've got a church to explore today."

Both filled their plates and carried on casual conversation while they devoured the food.

"I'll help you clean up," she said, picking up her plate.

"No need. I'll do it later. There's about a foot of snow on the roads and we should get going."

His voice was pleasant, but somehow guarded. She wondered if he was trying not to make her uncomfortable.

"I plowed the driveway so we shouldn't have any problems getting back to the highway. Want me to put the trunk in your car?"

She took the last sip of her Irish Coffee and nodded. "I don't think I have room in my trunk. After we leave the church, we can stop at the cafe and drop it off." A feeling of sadness came over her as she wondered how her mother would react.

He gave her a quick hug. "It will be okay. I'll stay with you when you tell your mom if you want me to."

She nodded and started walking back to the bedroom. "Let me get the box from the bedroom and I'll follow you to the church."

"I'll lock the front door when I go out. Just pull it closed after you."

Maggie walked quickly back to the bedroom, picked up the box, and walked back to the front room. She stopped briefly and looked around the log cabin. She felt an emptiness as if she were losing a longtime friend. She sighed and walked out the front door, making sure it was locked after her.

She followed Ethan's car to Summerhill. Her mind had cleared and her thoughts turned to Tony and what the key he left her opened. She listened to the radio and talked to herself, creating one scenario after another about what she awaited her at Trinity Lutheran Church. Her Bluetooth cell phone rang, snapping her back to reality.

"Hello?" she said.

"We'll be at the church in a few minutes. Did you call ahead or should I do that?"

Maggie smirked in the mirror. She was so busy daydreaming, she hadn't thought to call.

"I'll give them a call. I know the church secretary pretty well."

"Okay. I'll see you in the church parking lot."

"You bet," she answered ending the call.

She put her cell phone close to her mouth and said, "Call Mom". The phone promptly obeyed and her mother answered after the third ring.

"Maggie, thank goodness! I've been worried about you! What happened? When are you…"?

"Mom, I'm fine," she interrupted her in mid-sentence. "I have a lot to tell you, but now I need you to call Mable and see if we can…"

"WE?" it was her mom's turn to interrupt. "Who is with you?"

"It's the attorney," she answered, rolling her eyes and wishing she had chosen better words. "I need to get into Trinity. Will you call Mable at home and ask her to meet me at the church in twenty minutes?"

"Well, I guess so," her Mom said hesitantly. "I can't leave the cafe or I'd meet you there. What's going on?"

"Please, Mom, just call her. It's very important."

"All right. But I'm not happy about it."

"And Mom…" she paused. "I'm sorry you never had a chance to tell Tony goodbye."

"Tony? Tony Pontello? Did you see him?"

"I promise to explain, but I need you to call Mable right away."

"I will," her Mom's voice was shaking.

"Thanks," she replied and ended the call.

As she pulled into the church parking lot, Ethan was getting out of his car and Mable had pulled in behind him.

She parked the car and turned it off. She got out just in time to hear him speak to Mable.

"Hello. I'm Ethan Reynolds. Can you open the church for us? We need to find a Mr. Harvey Milner."

"Why do you need to speak to Harvey? He rarely has visitors."

Maggie hurried over to where they two were standing. "It's very important, Mrs. Vance, or I wouldn't ask you."

The older lady stood for a moment, looking from Maggie to Ethan and back several times.

"Margaret, I trust your mother and she wouldn't have asked me if it wasn't important." She paused. "Harvey's been suffering from dementia for years. He has good days and bad days. I'm not sure he will be able to speak with you." She pointed inside. "He comes to the church on his good days to pray. He's in the sanctuary now."

Maggie gave her a hug. "Thank you, Mrs. Vance."

She glanced at Ethan and motioned for him to follow her as she walked across the parking lot to the church entrance. She paused before opening the doors.

"I'm here for you," he said, putting his strong hand on her shoulders.

She smiled, opened the door and walked inside. The tiny church had twelve pews, six on either side of the center aisle. Three carpeted steps lead up to the altar. She'd never paid attention to the wood carvings until now. She had a strange feeling it was Tony's work.

"May I help you?" a male voice said from behind them.

Both turned to see a white-haired man dressed in overalls, wearing a necktie.

"I'm Maggie King and this is Ethan Reynolds. Are you Harvey Milner?"

The man silently walked toward them, using the pews to steady himself. He looked directly at her.

"Mr. Milner, did you know Tony Pontello?" Ethan asked politely.

The man stopped suddenly. His eyes never leaving Maggie's face.

CHAPTER 9

The man leaned his head to one side. Holding onto a pew with one hand, he slowly raised his other hand and touched Maggie's face.

Startled, she jerked and he put his hand down.

"You look so much like Tony," he remarked, stuttering slightly.

Ethan held on to her arm and steadied her. "How do you know Tony?"

"Mind if we sit down?" he asked.

"Of course," both answered at the same time.

"Tony hasn't come to visit me for a while," the man began. "He's gone home, hasn't he?"

Maggie and Ethan exchanged glances, not wanting to upset him.

"I'm Harvey," he said, "and I know he's gone home."

"How did you know Tony?" Ethan asked solemnly.

Harvey sat back in the pew and grinned. "I met Tony when the church hired him to make the altar. He never wanted anyone to watch him...but for some reason, he let me. Old Tony was my best friend. He was there for me when my wife died." The man looked down at his hands and a tear fell from his eyes.

"This pew," he said patting it, "was the last one he made. He suffered with great pain in his hands, but he finished it."

"Tony was like a father to me," Ethan began. "When my father died, he took me in."

Harvey nodded. "That sounds like Tony." Maggie's hand was holding onto the pew. He leaned forward and covered her hand with his.

"And he was your father, too," he smiled. "I tried to get him to contact you, but he was afraid his appearance would frighten you."

Maggie's voice cracked. "This is the first time I knew of him."

"It's all right," he said. "He wanted it that way. Suppose you have come to see what he left you."

"Well, yes. A key was left in a carved box for me." She suddenly look worried. "Oh, I left it in the car. Let me go…"

Harvey waved his hand. "No need. That lock has been changed many times since Tony left it in the box. We don't need it now."

She felt as if the wind had been knocked out of her. Ethan put his arm around her and looked at Harvey.

The man gave a chuckle. "Don't you want to see what he left you?"

The startled look on their faces made Harvey laugh louder. "It's in front of you."

They two turned around quickly. "Where? Is it in a closet or something?" Maggie asked.

"Help me stand up and I'll show you," Harvey said as he put his hand out for Ethan to grab. He stood and the three walked up the steps to face the altar.

"There's a hidden drawer built into the back of the altar. Tony put it there. He said it would be the safest place. You can get behind the altar from the right side. I'll guide you from there."

Her heart was in her throat as she and Ethan slid behind the altar. It was very close to the wall and their movement was limited.

"It's very tight back here," she called out.

"Tony meant for it to be. Look toward the middle. There should be square of wood that is a different color than the rest." He looked down at his feet. "Do you see it?"

"I see it," Ethan said loudly. "It's toward the top, right?"

"You'll need to look very hard for a dent in the upper left-hand corner. Push that and the wood will open."

"I can't reach it," Maggie said to Ethan. "Can you?"

He stood on tiptoe, grunted and scrapped his arm on the wall. Finally, he felt the dent. He made a fist and hit it. Nothing happened. He tried a few more times, but the square didn't move.

"It's so tight back here, I can't hit the square hard enough to open it," he shouted to Harvey, rubbing his fist. "Any other ideas?"

"Oh, I forgot the pocketknife," the man said, rubbing his forehead. "Do you have one?"

Ethan moved from behind the altar, checked his pockets and retrieved his small knife. "Always carry one!" he said as he went behind the altar once more.

He felt around the square, inserted the pocketknife and it fell off. He put his hand into the opening and pulled out a cloth bag.

He and Maggie wiggled out from behind the structure and he handed the bag to her.

Harvey was smiling broadly. "See, Tony. I kept it safe," he said looking up.

She untied the string holding the bag closed as fast as she

could. When the string fell to the ground, the contents of the bag spilled onto the carpet.

Maggie stood, staring few pieces of paper on the floor.

Ethan bent down to pick them up and carefully handed them to her.

"Good Lord!" she gasped. "These are stock certificates!"

She was speechless. Afraid to touch the yellowed papers and afraid to speak.

"Every time Tony built a pew, he would take most of the money he was paid and buy stock for you, Margaret." The old man smiled. "He told me if he couldn't be in your life, he would give you everything he had in his life. He was a good man."

Tears ran down her face. "He was a very good man."

ONE YEAR LATER

THE MUSIC BEGAN PLAYING AND ETHAN TURNED TO SEE Maggie coming toward him. She had left him breathless since the first time he saw her. She smiled and stood beside him, holding his hand tightly.

The high school band played as the Mayor of Summerhill motioned for them to come forward. As they approached, he raised his hand to stop the music and quieten the crowd.

"Welcome everyone. Thank you for coming! We are here to celebrate the Grand Opening of Tony's Family Tavern."

The crowd cheered and clapped.

"We are honored to have its owners, Ethan and Maggie Reynolds, here to cut the ceremonial ribbon to mark the official opening of the Tavern!" The crowd clapped and cheered louder.

"Which one of you is going to do the honors?" The Mayor asked holding a large pair of fake scissors.

"My lovely wife. Maggie." Ethan pulled her close and they shared a long kiss.

She took the scissors and the band played a drum roll as she cut the ribbon.

"Come in, everyone! Tony's Family Tavern is waiting to serve you! And if you are a veteran, your meal is always free."

ABOUT THE AUTHOR

Blessings to you! My name Laura Hern and I am pleased to meet you!

I've written in several genres including Cozy Mysteries, Romance, and NonFiction.

This short story, The Pew Maker, was written for a romance anthology called Kaleidoscope Hearts 3. It includes the stories of many award winning authors.

I hope you enjoy it!

My first series, a Cozy Mystery, is called the Lainey Maynard Mystery Series. I have always been an avid reader...and loved mysteries! I thought I was solving the cases with Sherlock Holmes, Nancy Drew, and Hercule Poirot. I love shows like Monk, psych, Midsomer Murders, and Miss Marple...they are fun, exciting, and cozy!

I love to hear from readers and look forward to sharing more adventures with you!

Laura

ALSO BY LAURA HERN

The Lainey Maynard Mystery Series

The Family Tree Murders - Book 1

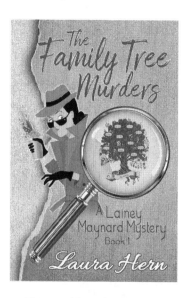

The email from her friend…

…had Lainey worried.

Why was Mary so upset over a DNA test?

Lainey needed a change after her husband's death. The quaint town of Mirror Falls, nestled among the lakes of northern Minnesota, was the perfect spot. She made some quirky friends. It was a restful life…

until the email.

Mary had done it as a lark. It might be fun to find out her family's history. When the DNA test came back, everything changed. The brother she loved was only her half-brother. And, it seemed, he was next in line for a substantial inheritance…

or murder.

As a successful insurance fraud investigator, Lainey had worked out more than her fair share of sinister plots, but this was different. With the help of her quirky friends, she's determined to figure out who's been trimming off branches of the family tree.

Will they find the murderer before he kills again?

You'll love this cozy mystery, because the characters are delightful, and the twists will keep you turning the pages.

Get it now.

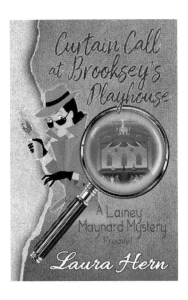

Curtain Call At Brooksey's Playhouse: The PREQUEL

Murder brought Lainey to Mirror Falls. Among the lakes and

forests of northern Minnesota, everything isn't as quaint as it seems. The local police captain isn't interested in her theories.

Who will she turn to?

Lainey's secret weapon is her brain and wit, but it's a double edge sword as her sassy mouth can get her in trouble. This time, though, it may be more than she can handle.

Chinese smuggling, jade mining, laundered money, and a double cross, lie at the heart of this delightful cozy mystery. You'll love every page, because Lainey is clever in all the right ways. *Get it now.*

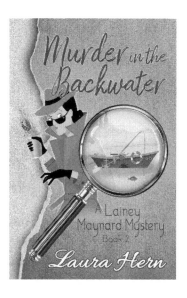

Murder In The Backwater: A Lainey Maynard Mystery Book 2

Everyone looked forward to it…

…the press swarmed the town.

Who knew fishing with stink bait could be deadly?

Lainey and her friends volunteered to help organize the fishing opener. It was supposed to be easy. Crowd control and a drawing of names. Nothing to it.

Things were going smoothly…

…until the dream.

Shep had always seen things. He'd gone to the police many times over the years, until they stopped listening. The town's people called him crazy. This time, Lainey believed him.

Would anyone else?

Her keen sense of intuition and cunning wit have served her well in the past. The more she digs, the more dirt piles up. This time, though, it may be more than she can handle. Could the town's favorite son, a former college football star, be involved?

Mistaken identities, smuggling, stink bait, and cat burglars lie at the heart of this delightful cozy mystery.

You'll love every page, because we all love the good guys to win in the end.

Get it now.

A nonfiction novel of love and loss that will break your heart while lifting your soul. Transplanted Faith is the amazing story of how God's love shines through even the darkest hour.

David, a faith-filled Christian man in his mid-forties, fought a two-year battle with Pulmonary Fibrosis, suffered through lung transplants, horrific complications, and financial loss, yet his faith in Jesus Christ never wavered.

In spite of the crushing blows of an incurable disease, Dave's faith was unwavering. This inspiring story of courage and love is a testament to the power of faith in the face of death.

Made in the USA
Monee, IL
15 April 2021